Dreamkeeper 20th

As winter ended and spring a   ___ .. world was unknowingly headed into a darkness that would be unprecedented in my lifetime. I was out on a multi-day trip flying around the country in a corporate jet, myself as captain, and my new friend Mark Lowe as first officer. Mark and I had only met a few days prior at the start of that rotation. Each day we did our job and tuned into the news as we watched the beginning of the Corona virus pandemic unfold before our eyes. When the word of the lockdowns got to us the whole world was stammered, wondering what the future held. I remember quite clearly sitting that evening with Mark as he showed me some amazing photographs he had taken of the night sky. Every photograph was more beautiful and awe inspiring than the last. Mark is a master of his craft, a true artist with a camera. Getting lost in the photos for a moment I remember thinking of an analogy. The stars are always there, shining brilliantly in the sky. It is only in the darkness of the night that they can be seen. Just like the friends and family that surrounded us during the darkness of the pandemic. Their light would shine through the darkness as brilliantly as the Milky Way on a moonless night. We got through it all together and the real stars did in fact shine, providing light for us all, staying kind and true and supportive. Thank you Mark for being one of those lights of hope and for letting me use your fantastic photograph to celebrate the 20th anniversary of my book Dreamkeeper.

Mark Lowe is a full-time flight/sim instructor and part-time photographer. His amazing prints are available on his website; marklowe.smugmug.com, or at www.instagram.com/marklowephotography.

By
Michael A. Rencavage

The original cover of Dreamkeeper is displayed here in memory of my old friend James (Jim) Rainey. Jim and I became friends as young men, when we worked at the local Kmart department store while in high school. Jim was an excellent guitar player and singer whose primary profession was that of a graphic artist responsible for advertising and marketing for a major supplement company. You may very well have seen his work at some point. Years later, as adults, Jim and I were standing on the sidelines while cheering for our youngest sons at a baseball game. I told him of a book project I was working on. Without the slightest hesitation, he volunteered to draw the cover. He was one of the kindest, nicest men I had ever met. A great husband and father with a quiet pleasant demeanor, Jim left us all too early due to an illness. God bless James Rainey and the family he left behind.

The author can be reached at:

Michael A. Rencavage

Mikethewriter53@gmail.com

Dreamkeeper 20th Anniversary Edition

Dreamkeeper was the first book I actually wrote. After reading "Propeller One Way Night Coach" by John Travolta, I decided that I wanted to write something for my son Christopher. I tossed around a few ideas and came to the conclusion that I would express some general philosophies and ideas to my then eight-year-old son with an aviation back drop to carry the story, as they say, write what you know.

The book came together pretty well as it gathered some little memories of the adventurous eight-year-olds' life in rural Pennsylvania coupled with a lesson or two about hanging on to your dreams and doing the work, about not being a victim and trying your best to be a part of the solution, not the problem.

The really cool thing was that for Christmas that year I was able to give Chris a copy of the book and the very first ever Dreamkeeper medallion. I had it made of silver and engraved and equipped to match the medallion in the story. He loved it, he still does.

It's twenty years later, and as time moved forward so many things have changed. I am no longer a first officer at an airline, but have found my home with Flexjet, a fractional ownership company for corporate jets. I have been a captain and instructor pilot and have enjoyed the best part of my career flying with a truly great company. Now, as I look forward and see less professional flying years ahead of me than behind me, my perspective has changed. I felt inspired in a different way by some of the newer pilots I had the opportunity to fly with. Speaking with the newer aviators in our company, I see that the dream of becoming a pilot is a bit different than it was when I was coming up, but it's still a big dream to many young aviators. I looked over the Dreamkeeper novella once more and made some changes. I even changed some of the highlighted experiences to reflect Chris' experiences as a teenager rather than an eight-year -old.

In my evaluation, I found that the people who pursue their passion are still out there chasing their dreams in pursuit of becoming an aviator or film maker, novelist, musician, engineer, entrepreneur, physician, or whatever lights their fire. (Tributary note to my wife's entrepreneurial endeavors and the candle business she is building from the ground up. (www.phriseilcandles com)) Many people are still working hard and rising to success even though they may have started from behind with little more than an idea and the drive and determination to make their idea a part of their reality. This book is really about that drive and determination, that ability to see a brighter future and pursue it. Dreamkeeper is written about a young aviator, however its' message transcends the limits of just one profession and applies to the dreamer in us all.

These days it seems that people who achieve their dream jobs often have to make a stop or two along the way to find the funding and support they need. I myself worked repairing and designing medical equipment until I could manage the career change at the ripe old age of 33. Twenty-five years later I am so thankful for the decades aloft and the friends and adventures that I never would have known had I not taken the chance and pursued my dream. The aviation industry is far better now, but the cost of entry is greater and only those who stick to it will see the rewards.

I hope my book helps some young would be aviators by sparking their interest and that it helps us older professionals to reflect upon what made us fall in love with flying so many years ago; that first flight or first solo or the thrill of taking your loved ones aloft for the first time. May it inspire the reader to take a moment to be grateful for what is and has been a great career aloft. It's easy to take it all for granted but when the blessings flow it's a good idea to count them once in a while with a grateful heart.

So, in closing, I'd like to say dream your big dream and never stop pursuing it. It's okay to take that good paying job in the other field, suffering for your art is not a prerequisite. It's better to chase dreams from your comfy home than to live in your car as a starving artist. The important thing is that you stay strong and look for the chance to do what you love while working everyday toward your goals. Write that screen play, sing at open mic night, star in that play, pen your novels or take the controls and soar through the sky. Success has so many meanings to so many people, find what works for you. Do the work! It's so worth it!

Best wishes,   Mike Rencavage
(mikethewriter53@gmail.com)

To Chris

All my love and respect, Dad

By
Michael A. Rencavage

1

Chris sat in the drive of his garage wrestling with the chain of his dirtbike. Earlier in the day the tire had gone flat and he had pushed the motorcycle the few remaining blocks to his house. Now, after a rather quick removal and repair of the rear inner tube, he was becoming frustrated with the reassembly.

All had gone well to this point, but the chain was putting up a fight. He couldn't seem to get it to roll into place on the rear sprocket , so he decided to pop the masterlink and try a different approach to the problem. Rising to his feet, he walked into the garage for a screwdriver.

The sound was incredible, a fierce roar like thunder passing behind him. It rumbled through the air, loud yet smooth and powerful. As he turned to see what it was, he was awestruck. There, no more than a hundred feet in the air, flew an antique biplane. The pilot sat proudly in its' open cockpit. It was as though he had appeared from nowhere, a time traveler perhaps or an angel just dropping by to say hello, able to disappear just as quickly as he arrived.

The site was magnificent. Just over the tops of the green summer trees, at the end of the long gravel drive, flew the bright white wings with gold and silver trim, glistening like sunbeams in the afternoon sky. The pilot waved and smiled as Chris returned the gesture with great enthusiasm, both arms flailing wildly.

Not more than a moment later, the thunder suddenly ceased. The loud smooth rumble was replaced by a series of rough coughs and spurts. The pilot, no longer waving, focused intensely straight ahead.

The hair on the back of Chris' neck stood up. He felt his muscles grow tense. He knew this couldn't possibly be good. Just moments ago he had witnessed the spectacular sight of an antique biplane flying proudly above the trees. Now that very same biplane was headed toward the ground, engine sputtering and finally stopping, the propeller standing still.

In all of Chris' 15 years he had never witnessed any sort of tragedy firsthand. His mind raced as his legs propelled him toward the line of trees and the field beyond. Would the pilot survive? What if there's a fire? What would he find on the other side of those trees?

13

Worried for the safety of the pilot, he ran faster and faster, digging in as if he were racing toward a finish line. Hurry, he thought, as he crossed the meadow and ran beneath the first row of thinly scattered trees. He dodged the last few rocks on the path and jumped the small stone wall. Clearing the row of pines, he saw him....

Bob Speranza was standing in front of the wing of his airplane. He was tall, at least six feet, maybe more, with dark hair cut short in a military style. He had inset hazel eyes and a strong athletic build, but most important, he was completely unharmed. He wasn't even the slightest bit shaken up by the event. He had survived the emergency without so much as breaking a sweat.

Bob's confidence was evident in everything he did, the way he stood, the way he walked. He strode calmly around the airplane examining it for possible damage. He feared that the rough terrain of the clearing might have harmed the airplane as it rolled to a stop. When he saw Chris sprinting from the woods he smiled and put up his hand, "It's all right kid, everything is all right." Chris stumbled to a stop in front of him. Bob went on, " I just had a little engine trouble, but I was never really in any danger. This old plane glides pretty well and the field here was a near perfect place to land, a little rough, but plenty long."

His heart pounding, gasping for air, Chris started to speak, "I....I thought you might be in trouble." Bob turned back toward the plane, "No trouble kid, that is as long as the owner of this field isn't too upset." Chris had finally caught his breath. Standing with his hands on his knees, he looked up through the dark brown hair that had fallen in his eyes, "Mr. Pilger won't mind. He's in Illinois visiting his family. He won't be back for at least two days."

Bob stared for a moment at the large radial engine, its chrome reflecting the afternoon sun. "I'm going to need some tools, kid. Do you think you could help me with that?" Chris sprang to his feet, "Sure can, I've got a whole garage full of tools just beyond those trees."

15

They walked together back to the garage and Chris bombarded Bob with questions. "What's it like to fly? How fast do you go? Is it safe?" Bob loved to fly and to talk about flying. He graciously replied to each and every question one by one. Bob had a very special quality, a certain knack for explaining things that brought the conversation to a level that anyone involved could understand. He and Chris talked for hours as they retrieved the tools and started the repairs on the biplane. Chris watched and listened intently, gleaning every ounce of information he could from this stranger that had fallen from the sky.

"Hey, Chris, hold this wrench, that's it." Bob turned the final bolt and sighed, "That should just about do it." He wiped the sweat from his brow with his forearm and smiled. "Well, kid, I'd sure like to repay your kindness with a ride, but it's getting dark and I have to be at my friend's farm before sunset. No lights on these older ones, ya know."

Bob handed Chris the wrench, "I do have something I'd like to give you." He reached into the front cockpit and grabbed his flight bag. From the bottom of the bag, way back, he pulled out a small, circular, silver medallion. It was about one inch in diameter and looked rather antique with lots of swirled engravings on the front. In the center was a fancy letter "**D**".

They leaned against the lower wing and Bob handed the medallion to Chris. "I want you to have this." Chris took it into his hand letting the chain dangle between his thumb and forefinger. "What is it?" Turning away once more to place his flight bag back in the airplane, Bob replied. "It's a dreamkeeper medallion." "A what?" asked Chris. Bob leaned back and folded his arms. "Kid, you'll often hear a man referred to as a dreamer. People say that today as though it were a negative thing, something to be looked down upon. I can't express to you strongly

16

enough just how wrong that is. Some of the most important things in our lives are our dreams, you know, goals and ambitions." Bob turned and looked Chris directly in the eyes. "If you have a dream, you immediately transform yourself from a victim of circumstance to an adventurer of life. Dreams empower a person, making them instantly victorious over the everyday drudgeries of their existence. Even the harshest of conditions become nothing more than a test, a trial that you must pass through along the way to fulfilling your dream.

Dreams are responsible for so many wonderful things. Just look at my airplane for instance, if not for the dreams of a couple of bicycle mechanics in the early part of the twentieth century, we may never have known the wonders of flight."

Chris paused for a moment, staring at the medallion in his hand. "So what does this have to do with my dreams?" Bob leaned forward, "As I said, this is a dreamkeeper medallion. Every night just after you say your prayers and before you fall asleep, you hold this medallion in your right hand. Then close your eyes and think of your dream. Picture yourself doing exactly what it is you dream of doing. I personally guarantee that, over time, your dream will become your reality."

Chris looked up at Bob with wide eyes and said, "But don't you need it?" Bob replied, "Not anymore. Once you've figured out the secret of its power, you no longer need the medallion itself. The medallion is just a tool to get you started until, in your own way, you unlock its secret." Bob took the medallion from Chris' hand and placed it around his neck. "Good luck kid, and thanks again."

17

Chris threw the box of tools on his shoulder and started back toward the garage. He turned and watched as Bob started the engine.

  The propeller started to spin, slowly at first, then faster and faster. With a great puff of bluish-white smoke, the huge radial engine coughed to life, shattering the silence of the evening field with an overwhelming roar of thunderous horsepower. Bob waved from the rear seat and turned the airplane around, taxiing it to the edge of the clearing. The sound grew louder and louder and louder! Then suddenly, this mass of noise and steel and wood and fabric lifted off more gracefully than any bird that Chris had ever seen.

Chris waved once more as the majestic old biplane faded away into the crimson sky of a beautiful summer evening.

By
Michael A. Rencavage

2

In the garage once more Chris put away his tools, wiping each one clean with a red cotton cloth and placing it back in its' appropriate spot in his tool case. He took good care of everything he owned, a habit he had picked up from his father. He knew his family had certain financial limitations and that replacing lost or broken items could take time and extra money that they really didn't have. The blue and white Yamaha sat in the corner, repairs completed, readied for tomorrow's ride.

Chris turned to see the lights of the maroon minivan flooding the drive. They drew closer and closer, finally coming to a stop in the far bay of the garage. The lights went out and the rear hatch of the van opened automatically as a small aluminum ramp lowered gently to the ground. It always reminded Chris of the batmobile, sleek smooth automation. It's purpose was a bit more functional he thought, as his mom and brother exited through the rear of the vehicle and restored it to its normal boring appearance with the touch of a button on the remote.

Michael had been unable to walk for as long as Chris could remember. In fact he was never able to walk. He has cerebral palsy, a disease that affects the ability of the brain to control the body.

He was a handsome young man, five years Chris' senior with light brown hair and hazel eyes. He had the most memorable laugh of anyone Chris had ever met. A hearty giggle with a smile from one end of his dimpled face to the other. He had his mother's lighter coloring, but sitting there next to his dad he looked like a younger model of the same design. Michael's speech came from a device that was attached to his wheelchair. "Hi Chris!" he said in the voice of a youthful robot. Chris replied, "Hi Mike, did you have fun with mom and dad?" Mike turned the corner and climbed the ramp into the house in his electric wheel chair. "Sure did, I'll see you inside.", he said.

Chris turned to his mom and gave her a hug to greet her. She asked how his day was and he told her it was incredible! His mom headed inside as well while his father called from the rear of the van. " Is your dirt bike fixed?"

"Yeah, It was a bit of a struggle, but in the end it's all back together. " said Chris.

" How about spending a little time helping me with my Scrambler? "

A scrambler is similar to a street motorcycle but with a raised exhaust pipe, reinforced handlebars, knobby tires and some additional protection equipment like a mesh light guard and a skid plate to protect the light and engine from rocks on the trail. Chris's dads' bike was given to him as payment for helping an elderly family friend install a new engine in a very old car. The man had limited money so Big Mike, as Chris's dad was called, did the work for free. When the job was done the elderly man insisted that Big Mike keep his scrambler, a motorcycle he had quit riding some time ago, as payment for Mike's hard work. Gratitude seems to come in many forms and now Big Mike was the one who was grateful. Big Mike had torn down the whole motorcycle and repainted it, then he rebuilt the engine from the ground up. It was nearly ready to ride, with just a few minor things to tidy up before its' maiden voyage, so to speak.

Chris and his dad, Big Mike, grabbed a flashlight from the wall of the garage and walked together toward the large shed in the backyard. Once there, Big Mike unlocked the door and flipped on the lights. The metallic blue scrambler looked like new as it sat perched in the motorcycle lift. Together they made the final adjustments to the freshly cleaned carburetor and installed it on the bike. As they worked, they talked, and

Chris shared the incredible story of his day. Big Mike was mesmerized by what his son was telling him. They spoke well into the night as they readied the motorcycle for its first start in 25 years.

Chris and his father were always very close. To this day, they share everything, from the color of their hair and eyes to an overall enthusiasm for life.

Just before his dad jumped on the kickstarter, he came up with what would be the question of the night. " If this medallion empowers you to fulfill your dreams and make them a reality, what is it that you choose to do?" Chris was silent for a moment, surprised at first by the question.

"I'm not sure, Dad, but I'll think of something."

Big Mike jumped on the kickstarter twice and on the second kick the old engine roared to life. In minutes they had tweaked the carburetor, adjusting the idle and airflow to make it run smoothly.

That night Chris lay awake in bed looking through his window at the rising moon shining brightly in full glory, its light gently illuminating the bedroom walls. Clutched firmly in his right hand was his new treasured possession. He fell asleep pondering his father's question, taking very seriously the decision he was about to make.

By
Michael A. Rencavage

3

Three months had passed since the day Bob had given Chris the medallion. Each night he pondered his father's question. He searched his heart, as so many young people do, looking for a clue as to what it was that he wanted to do with his life, what path he would choose. Chris was an avid reader and after the encounter with Bob Speranza he started to read aviation-based books to understand more of why people become pilots. He was inspired by the writings of St. Exupery a French aviator and author from the 1920s 30s and 40s. In his book "Night Flight", St.Ex wrote of choosing a life that was equal parts adventure and contemplation! Aviation offered both and Chris dreamed of grand adventures in the air and on distant lands. The thought of intellectual pursuits intrigued him as well. Perhaps writing or engineering held some merit. After months of contemplation, it was the works of Richard Bach that truly inspired Chris. Within Bach's writing Chris fell in love with flying. He had never even flown in an airplane yet and looking at it from outside the fence at the airport he couldn't imagine how he would ever join the ranks of those who flew. He thought the act of flying was reserved for people whose families were pilots or who knew someone in aviation. Still, he felt an amazing draw toward flight as he read the great authors of adventure aloft. Bach, St. Ex, Lindbergh, Earnest Gann. He found each book more intriguing than the other and in time his future became a vision that he could imagine, a dream that he could see clearly in his mind's eye.

Chris was covered with spatters of mud from head to toe. A late-night rainstorm had left the trails quite wet and the puddles were all but unavoidable. Not that a fifteen- year-old boy would have any interest in avoiding them anyway. He grabbed an ice cold bottle of water from the fridge and exchanged his helmet and riding boots for a beat up old pair of sneakers. "Hey, Mom, I'm heading out!" he yelled, as the screen door slammed behind him and he ran across the yard to the field next door. Climbing the apple-tree he stretched out his arm and nabbed a juicy red apple from the limb above his head. Chris sat quietly now, his legs

24

dangling carefree from a branch as his shoulders pressed back against the trunk of the tree.

He leaned his head back and peered through an open area in the branches. The crisp blue sky was sliced with two parallel lines of white clouds, contrails created as the moisture in the air turned into ice crystals, leaving behind the evidence of a passing jetliner. He smiled to himself, feeling comfortable and relaxed as he took a swig of his water to wash down a bite of apple.

Sue came running down the path and stopped at the base of the tree. She was a thin girl with golden hair, beautiful blue eyes and a smile that charmed anyone who spoke to her. She was also Chris' best friend. They were inseparable since the third grade. They were always happy to see each other. Chris felt she understood him better than anyone. The fact that she lived just a few houses down on the same street kept their visits frequent and often long.

She stood at the foot of the tree with her hands stuffed in the front pockets of her faded blue jeans and looked up shyly at Chris.

"Hey, what's up?"

Chris was happy to see her, he was anxious to tell her of his recent decision, sparked by his reading and his encounter with Bob, and to show her once again the medallion. He felt as though it held the key to his future. He removed the medallion, handing it carefully to Sue. She thought it was absolutely beautiful and gazed at it a while, studying the design before returning it. "Wow!" she said. "That really is amazing , do you have any idea what your first dream will be?" Chris leaned his head back once more and stared at the contrails.

"I've been thinking about it long and hard ever since Bob gave me the medallion and I think I've finally decided." Chris took another swig of water, swallowing with a gulp. "I've always liked airplanes, and the stories that Bob had told me of the challenge and adventure of flight really hit home with me. I have tossed the question of which dream, which future I should chose around in my mind time and time again. Each time I came up with the same answer... I want to be a pilot.

I just think it would be the greatest thing ever to spend your life traveling from city to city exploring the world. Just imagine riding high above the clouds, soaring through the sky, sunsets at altitude and full circle rainbows."

Sue stepped back, "Full circle rainbows?" "Yeah" said Chris, "Bob told me that if you fly straight at a rainbow at altitude the rainbow wraps completely around the airplane. He's seen it twice and said it's truly spectacular." Sue smiled, "Just promise me that I'll be your first passenger." Chris jumped from the tree and shook her hand. Then hugged her gently. "It's a deal."

They walked together back to Chris' house arriving just in time for dinner, after which they played some video games, laughing and joking until well after dark. Sue stood up and stretched, "I'd better be heading home." Chris jumped to his feet stumbling a bit to catch his balance, "I'll walk you."

26

They strolled slowly down the dark country road gazing at the evening sky. Without the ambient light of the city, the stars sparkled so brightly, twinkling like diamonds in the clean country air. Out of the silence Sue started to speak, "You know, when you're traveling all over the world, I'm going to miss you." Chris replied in a calm and soothing voice," I'll miss you, too, but I have an idea." He pointed to the night sky. "See the big dipper, that group of stars that make up a huge cup and handle?" Sue nodded acknowledgment and he continued. "Now see the star in the upper right corner of the cup?" Another nod, "Yes." "That will be our star. The evening sky will be our link to one another. No matter where we are, we need only to look at our star and remember each other. That star will always remind me of your smile." Sue smiled, "That's so thoughtful."

She gently bit her lower lip and glanced downward trying to hide what she was feeling for Chris. They said good night on the front walk and Chris waited, watching over her until she was safely inside.

He sprinted all the way home, bursting through the door and startling his dad who was enjoying a hot cup of coffee at the kitchen table. After catching his breath, Chris filled him in on the choice he had made that day. His father stood up smiling, "If that's your dream, Chris, we'll do everything in our power to help you make it come true."

Later that night, lying, in bed Chris did exactly as Bob had said and fell asleep with the small silver medallion held firmly in his right hand.

By
Michael A. Rencavage

4

Chris was never really a morning person and today was no exception. The last one to awaken in the house, he rose to the smell of simmering bacon and dragged his weary body to the kitchen. While eating breakfast with his family, his father asked what his plans were for the rest of the morning. "I don't really have any, Dad, Why, do you need my help with something?" "Yes," his dad said, "I need you to come with me as soon as you can get dressed."

Chris finished his eggs and showered. He threw on his work jeans and an old T-shirt with a faded American Flag emblazoned on the front. He was anticipating a bit of manual labor by the nature of his father's request.

His dad was waiting patiently in the minivan when he exited the front door of the house. "Sorry, Mom!" he yelled, and he winced as the screen door slammed behind him. Chris jumped in, being just slightly gentler with the door of the minivan. "Where are we going, Dad?" "You'll see when we get there," his father replied. The van eased backward over the long gravel drive, then turned and disappeared in the sunlight, eastbound on Center Street.

As they crested the hill on Route 435, Chris' eyes were fixed out the right window. They had driven by the Daleville airport many times in the past, but now it took on a whole new meaning in Chris' life.

He studied the skies intently, scanning for any signs of aircraft in flight, excited about his new dream. Chris was pleasantly surprised when his father pulled off the two lane and onto Airport Road.

At the end of the drive, they parked between an old trailer and a brand new convertible with its top down exposing the white leather interior. Chris opened his door cautiously to avoid scraping the paint on the arrest me red Corvette.

He paused for a moment taking in the sites. A group of small airplanes were tied down all along the eastern side of the field, beyond them were two rows of blue and white hangars. The airport had a grass runway, about one half of a mile in length and groomed to perfection. A narrow strip of dirt marked the area where the planes actually landed and rolled out. There were trees on the opposite side in what seemed like an exceptionally neat row and a bright orange windsock hanging limp in the calm morning air. Just in front of the trailer was a set of fuel pumps and a dirt path that led to the runway.

The taxiway, Chris thought, as he heard the little Cessna approaching from the southwest. He watched as the pilot gently touched the wheels to the ground. The main wheels touched first, then the nose, and a sudden burst of power took him back into the air for another circuit. Chris ran to catch up with his father and they walked inside to speak with the owner and arrange for his first flight lesson.

When Chris stepped outside the trailer again he met the man that would be his flight instructor. A gray haired gentleman of average build, Bill Beichler appeared to be in his mid 50's. He seemed to have a certain kindness about him that exuded from his youthful personality. Chris took to him immediately. They shook hands and introduced themselves.

31

Bill was a school teacher by trade but loved to fly so much that he instructed students in the evenings and on weekends just for fun. He enjoyed sharing the experience he had gained in some 30 years of flying. They became acquainted as they walked across the field together toward the line of airplanes.

The morning dew made Chris' sneakers wet as they untied the orange and white Cessna. The nylon ropes were used to hold it firmly to the ground in the event of a storm. Bill turned to Chris and said, "You couldn't have chosen a better day for a first flight." He was right, of course. Chris looked up at a sky that was completely cloud free, clear blue for as far as the eye could see, horizon to horizon. There was no more than a gentle breeze from the northeast. It was certainly as near perfect as one could possibly expect.

As they walked around the plane Bill explained the finer points of a good preflight inspection. Chris studied every detail of the craft. He thought it amazing that all of this aluminum and steel and plastic was going to be able to leave the ground at all. It looked awfully heavy for a magic carpet.

Inspection complete, they slid into their appropriate seats, Bill on the right, and Chris on the left enjoying the captain's perspective. Chris was overwhelmed, he couldn't believe that this was actually going to happen. He held his medallion for a second thinking wow, this thing really does work.

After carefully completing all of the items on the checklist, Chris cautiously turned the key to the start position and the little airplane

rumbled to life. It was nothing like the sound of Bob Speranzas'
Stearman but that smooth steady rumble was magical nonetheless.

They taxied to the southwest end of the runway for departure and
completed yet another checklist. Chris brought the power up smoothly
to test the engine, just as Bill had said. In a flash he felt flooded with fear.
His knees were actually quivering as he held the brakes, thoughts were
racing through his mind. I've never left the ground before. Is this really
safe? Will I ever know what to do with all of these gauges? He calmed
himself thinking, you're in good hands, just settle down and give it a try.
As he brought the power back to idle he took a deep breath and tried to
relax.

About that time Bill said, "Well, we're all ready, taxi it out to the center
of the strip and I'll take care of the radios." Chris gently added power
and zig zagged a bit as he became accustomed to steering with his feet.

Once they were lined up Bill turned again to Chris, "Give her hell."
Chris pushed the throttle full forward and the plane began to accelerate.
He struggled to keep it straight. The pedals seemed oversensitive to his
touch as he careened again from left to right and back toward center
going faster and faster down the runway. At just about the middle of the
field Bill said in a calm and confident voice, "Okay, now ease back gently
on the stick, a little more, a little more…" The little airplane lifted off
using all its might to climb away from the earth at the command of
gentle back pressure from a fledgling pilot.

Chris couldn't believe it. He yelled to Bill over the roar of the engine, "I
did that?" Bill replied, "You sure did." At that very moment all of the
fear and anticipation disappeared and Chris fell in love with flying.

The view was spectacular as he looked down on the fields and trees and the houses of the small town that had been his home for his entire life. It all looked so different, so small. The scene reminded him of Christmas at his grandmother's house. The town was reminiscent of the train platform he loved to help assemble every year. What an intense feeling it was, the freedom to move in any direction he chose, up, down, side to side. It was breathtaking, the view from the air, the sound of the engine, that glorious feeling of freedom. What could possibly be better than this? He held the medallion once more and smiled to himself.

They spent the remainder of the hour flying around the practice area getting the feel of the aircraft in flight. Climbs, descents, turns, Chris concentrated intensely as he tried to make the airplane comply with the requests of his instructor. Bill coached him as he flew out over his house and circled the small green ranch with the slate roof and his mother waiving from the back porch. He rocked the wings to acknowledge her and then worked his way back toward the airport where Bill took over for the landing.

Walking back into the trailer, Chris was one giant 15 year old smile. His ears were blocked from the changes in air pressure and he unknowingly spoke rather loudly, like when you try to have a conversation without removing your earbuds.

They sat for a moment with his dad and Dave Carver , the owner of the airport. Chris and his father began to discuss his ambitions with Bill and Mr. Carver.

As the conversation proceeded the mood of the room fell sharply from the joy of a first flight toward the sullen demeanor of broken dreams.

Chris watched his father's face sadden upon hearing the cost of bringing Chris' dream to reality. There would be several flying ratings to achieve, a college degree and years of attaining the experience required to become a professional pilot. The total would run somewhere in the neighborhood of $200,000 a sum unimaginable to Chris and his family. It would be in excess of what they had paid for their home. They spoke momentarily about the military, but Chris' reading glasses would eliminate any chance of becoming a military pilot.

They left the trailer a lot less excited than when they had arrived. Chris was certain that his father could never afford all of that. His father was only an auto mechanic with an income that was barely enough to get by on, let alone pay for this dream of Chris'. They talked quietly on the way home as Chris described his experience in the air, knowing that it might just be the last chance he would ever have to fly an airplane.

That night Chris lay in bed, eyes wide open staring through the window as droplets of rain dripped slowly toward the sill. The moonlight was obscured by the gray overcast sky. What good was this medallion anyway? It gave him a dream only to crush it moments after it came to life. As his eyes started to fill with tears, he remembered Bob's words. "If you have a dream you immediately transform yourself from a victim of circumstance to an adventurer of life. Dreams empower a person, making them instantly victorious over the everyday drudgeries of their existence. Even the harshest of conditions become nothing more than a test, a trial that you must pass through along the way to fulfilling your dream. "

Chris once again held his medallion tightly, closed his eyes for a moment and pictured himself flying. When he opened them he noticed a glimpse of the moon shining through a break in the clouds.

He knew in his heart that Bob would not have steered him wrong, that someday, someway his dream would come true. If life was going to present him with a test, he was certainly going to pass it. He wiped his eyes and rolled over, reaffirmed in his faith, falling peacefully off to sleep.

By
Michael A. Rencavage

5

A few months had passed since that night when Chris declared to himself his determination. Each night he did exactly as Bob had said, he said his prayers, held his medallion, envisioned his dream and fell away to sleep.

Not too much had changed though. Chris had taken a morning paper route and a job at the local grocery store. He delivered the news before dawn and spent his evenings and weekends stocking shelves, gathering shopping carts , and sweeping floors. It provided him with enough money for a flight lesson every two months. That was far too infrequent and the progress was slow, but it did help to keep his dream alive. He would purchase the books he needed with whatever cash he had left at the end of each lesson. His dad had bought him a flight computer and a log book, providing him with some necessary tools to help prepare him for the future. Things were moving ahead, but the pace was excruciatingly slow.

Chris pulled in the clutch with his left hand as his right foot slammed on the brake. The rear wheel of the Yamaha slid forward trying to catch the front as the loose dirt from the path sprayed into the air. Chris stopped the bike only momentarily, then down shifted and proceeded, letting the clutch out slowly. The path had narrowed and led to a small steel bridge that spanned the creek some twenty feet in the air. He glanced back to see his dad and the scrambler emerging from his cloud of dust. Then he carefully crossed the old bridge dodging the missing plank and glimpsing down momentarily as the water ran below the gaping hole that passed to his left.

The double track was rough and pocked with one mud puddle after another. Skimming the edges of the huge puddles, Chris steered his bike back and forth avoiding the roughest of the terrain like a slalom racer on a highspeed downhill. He was focused and relaxed all at the same time.

38

His mind concentrated as his body let the motorcycle flow with the everchanging terrain. His father was nipping at his heels as they approached the bottom of the long rocky hill that led to the top of Dam number 5, the city's water supply reservoir. Chris opened the throttle and the powerful 250 cc dirt bike jumped the final rock, landing in the clearing at the top and sliding sideways then slowing.

The clearing was wide open. Chris bore to the left and idled slowly toward the line of trees, finally coming to a stop. He fiddled for a moment with the gear shifter until a little green light on the speedometer indicated that he had found the neutral position, then he lowered the kickstand and flipped the little red switch beneath his right thumb. The constant thump of the engine stopped almost immediately as his dad pulled in behind him.

Chris took off his helmet and placed his riding gloves inside, then hung it safely on the handle bar. Big Mike finished the hill climb with a bit less flare merely rolling gently over the final lip of the hill after steering around the rocks that Chris had jumped. He rolled slowly to a stop next to Chris, finding neutral then bringing the sounds of nature to the forefront as he clicked off the scrambler's ignition key and his bike fell silent.

Big Mike removed his riding gear and laid it across the seat of his bike, he was smiling from ear to ear, he really enjoyed his Father's Day rides with Chris. It was an annual tradition that they both tried never to miss.

Chris was staring at the rock wall and the back side of the well house in disbelief. What once was an idyllic setting off in the middle of the woods, had somehow been corrupted. Chris looked at his dad and said,

" I can't believe someone would come to such a beautiful place and make the effort to carry along a paint can to write profanity and tag their initials in a multi colored graffiti fest. Not even an artistic drawing, just words on a wall that brought the hood into the woods. That's terrible." Chris was struck with disgust, staring at the worthless efforts of basically a vandal in the wilderness. His dad stepped up behind him and placed his hand on Chris's shoulder., "Come on son I've got lunch, maybe the next time we come here we can bring along something to start cleaning this stuff off and make it right again."

They climbed the stone wall together and perched themselves on top. Big Mike opened his back pack and pulled out two huge Italian subs, two bags of chips and two bottles of iced tea. They sat and ate atop a wall that was made nearly a hundred years before their mountain lunch looking out at the pristine view.

The reservoir was true serenity not a single sound was present except for the sounds of nature itself. Sitting in silence Big Mike closed his eyes and leaned his head back. From the right he heard the peaceful flowing of water running over the top of the Dam as it made it's way to the creek some 80 feet below. It was a cascading, soothing, constant flow that pleased the ears and could let you drift softly into an almost meditative state. The birds chirped from the forrest trees that surrounded the pristine reservoir. Mike opened his eyes to see the sun glistening off the gentle ripples of the water. He breathed deeply the crisp clean air and sighed, "This is living kid." When he looked toward Chris, Big Mike expected to see some type of relaxed peaceful smile, instead he could feel the tension emanating from his son. He asked what was wrong.

Chris replied," It's mostly just this whole flying thing. It's moving so slowly that I can't help but be frustrated. Every day I work toward my goals and every day I feel the frustration of my limitations. It doesn't look like I'll ever get to where I want to be."

"That is difficult to overcome son, but, it's important to keep the right perspective. Let me tell you a little story.:

Your mom and I had spent many a summer's evenings hiking along the waterfalls at Ricketts Glen. Nearly every time we went, we would see this very athletic young woman who seemed to always choose the same time we did to traverse the falls loop. We walked briskly together but the young girl was always hiking at a furious pace. She would blow by us with nothing more than an "On your right!" Uttered as she passed. One day as we came to Canoga falls, at the base of the falls, where the water pooled, was a doe with two young fawns sipping water. They were surrounded by lush green flora with a rainbow arcing over them in the distance. The sight was spectacular! We quietly took a picture then slid away so as not to startle them. Minutes later we were at the top of the trail entering the parking lot and we ran into the young athlete. She had passed us just after our stop for that wonderful moment in nature. When I approached her and mentioned the majestic scene she looked at me sternly stating that she was training for a nature run and didn't have the time for such nonsense. She was training for a Nature Run! And she had no time to observe Nature! Amazing! She didn't take kindly to my chuckle, but I found it to be a spectacular set of circumstances. I bring that up just to share with you the importance of your perspective. Don't get so caught up in your goals that you miss out on life.

Life is meant to be lived and enjoyed. "

41

Chris grinned and looked toward his dad, "Dad your life is far from everything you imagined, yet somehow you are almost always in a good mood."

"Well son your brother has a lot to do with that, "said Big Mike.

"The first year after we had Mikey, he was in and out of the hospital on ventilators and struggling to survive over and over again. Watching him suffer so much for that whole year was excruciating. It was the most stressful time of my life. Right around his first birthday, after multiple ER visits and hospital stays and countless prayers, Mikey stopped needing intervention. His lungs and immune system developed to that of a normal one year old and as quickly as it had begun, our year of suffering ended. He is hardly ever ill these days. After that I developed a motto. As long as nobody in the family is sick or dying, it's a good day! What I'm saying is that I sympathize with your struggle, and I am sure you'll get through and make it to your goals.

In the meantime, keep your chin up. Don't spend all of your time focused on the problem. It's like our view right here. This lake is a flashback to my childhood. Today we got here on two awesome motorcycles. When I was a kid we hiked for hours to get here to sneak a swim and have a sandwich. Today it's much the same as it used to be, nearly frozen in time. The only difference is that dang graffiti fest someone had on the other side of the wall. Come with me a minute."

They packed the remnants of their lunch into the back pack and jumped back down off the wall , walking back toward the bikes, Big Mike stopped and turned once more toward the lake. Placing his right hand on Chris's left shoulder he said, " It's all here at the same time son, the

42

good and the bad! It's what you bring to it that makes the difference in your day. It's what you focus on. Look up and there it is, the most beautiful lake in the state, serene, with just a gentle ripple that reflects the sunlight as the water flows toward the falls. Listen to the water cascading across the stones of the falls. Soak up the flora, the majestic oak trees leaning toward the water's edge. Listen to the birds chirping. This is one spectacular view! Looking out you can take it all in. Or, you can keep your head down staring at the graffiti left by some ignorant person who missed the whole point of being here. The graffiti and the lake are both here at the same time. Whatever you choose to focus on will have a significant impact on how you view your day. You and I will find the way to overcome the obstacles and you will build the life you choose. As for me, right now I am going to look at the lake, look at all that natural beauty! Look at that rope swing, someone left a rope swing over there hanging from that oak tree! Now that's. Awesome! Let's go!"

Chris and Big Mike always wore their bathing suits under their riding pants when they came to the lake so as to be able to take a dip and cool off from their ride in the sun. The rope swing was an added bonus. They quickly stripped down to their swim suits and dashed across the shallow water at the top of the dam. Chris grabbed the rope and stepped back as far as he could then swung out into the deep water in front of the giant rock letting go and splashing down nearly twenty feet from shore. Big Mike grabbed the rope as quickly as it had returned and in a flashback to his youth followed suit with Chris. It was cold and refreshing. They swam for a while together then returned to the bikes and got geared up for the soggy ride home.

Chris looked out over the lake once more and said, "I choose the lake over the graffiti. I have to remember to put that thought to work for me." It's a good way to go through life, the right perspective makes for a pretty good day! His dad smiled, "let's go meet Mikey and head to our Father's Day movie."

His afternoon and dinner was spent with his family and after a full day of homespun adventures, Chris walked the few hundred yards to Sues' house. There he spent the evening with her watching a movie until she fell asleep with her head resting on his chest. They were finally dating after years of friendship and this was one part of his life that Chris felt comfortable with. He belonged with Sue he had known that for years , she did too. One night after work, Sue showed up to walk home with Chris. They kissed for the first time on her front porch and had been dating ever since.

With Sue sleeping peacefully in his arms, Chris clicked off the TV and spent a few moments lost in his thoughts by the light of the fireplace. He really liked the words of wisdom his father had shared. He thought of them as he reflected upon his day. He began to try and come up with some sort of plan to help keep his dreams on track. Almost subconsciously he held the dreamkeeper medallion between his thumb and fore finger as he thought of Bob Speranza and the day they met under circumstances that felt like nothing less than divine intervention. He kept trying to find a way to take the next step.

The pursuit of his dream was something he enjoyed, but the pace he was keeping would not produce the desired outcome.

When Chris started first grade his father had told the worried seven year old "Just relax, son, as long as you do your best, that's what truly matters." Chris was thinking of that and pondering whether or not there was something more he could do. He had learned at a very young age to look to himself for solutions first, then ask for help if necessary. This philosophy often brought a certain amount of pride when he presented his parents with solutions rather than just problems.

He was suddenly struck with an idea. He would be able to get at least three thousand dollars for his dirt bike. That, combined with the money he earned would get him to the point of his first solo and bring him up to a lesson every week or two. This would be great, he thought. He could sell his bike to the local Yamaha dealer and be on a regular flying schedule by the weekend.

He realized he would be giving up one of the things he enjoyed most in life, but the sacrifice would be an investment in his future. It would take him to the point of becoming a pilot, a label he felt could only be worn once he had flown the airplane solo, with nobody there to back him up or bail him out.

The next afternoon Chris stopped by the motorcycle shop between school and work. His estimate was correct. He left the shop counting his cash and planning his next flight lesson. He stopped for a moment and called Bill to set up an appointment. He couldn't wait until he got home to tell his dad the good news. Chris walked to work whistling to himself, something he only seemed to do if he was nervous or happy. Today the latter was the case.

That evening Chris strolled into the driveway of his home grinning from ear to ear when his dad arrived from work sporting pretty much the same expression. The van came to a stop and his dad stepped out yelling to Chris. "Hey, Chris, I've got some great news." Chris replied, "So do I." His dad was beaming with excitement, but he could tell Chris was just as enthusiastic. "You first," said his dad. Chris smiled proudly and told him what he had done with the motorcycle. His father said, "That's great, Chris, but you didn't have to do that. I spoke to my boss at work and they approved overtime all the way though to next fall. I signed up to work Saturdays. That would give us enough money to afford a flight lesson every week or two. That should help you get started."

Chris couldn't believe his ears, things were really going to start moving along. "That's great news, Dad, thank you so much." Chris' dad glanced down at the cash in his hand then began to speak, "Can you get your bike back? You won't need that money right now." Chris replied sadly, "No, he was selling it as I was leaving the shop." His dad smiled once more, " Well, I want you to keep that money, put it in the bank. We still have a long way to go to make that dream of yours a reality." They walked together into the house and Chris rushed to the phone to call Sue and let her in on the good news.

By
Michael A. Rencavage

6

Chris sat alone now on the grass runway at the Daleville airport, not so much nervous as focused. After months of training the time had finally come. Mr.Beichler had flown the traffic pattern twice with him that morning to be sure he was on his game. Everything went well and he asked Chris to taxi over to the fuel pumps and let him out. With a handshake for both luck and affirmation of his faith in the young pilot, Mr. Beichler stepped from the plane. Chris taxied away alone for the very first time.

Chris had turned sixteen just yesterday. Recently, he had been focusing all of his time and energy on flying. This was the day, the day every pilot remembers for the rest of their life. It was all up to him now. He alone would be responsible to launch the little Cessna into the sky and return safely without anyone else there to help him.

He had completed the checklists and sat ready at the beginning of the runway. Chris was sure that he was capable or Mr. Beichler would never have put him in this situation. The only fear he had was that he would panic or choke as athletes called it.

He focused his attention down the runway and smoothly brought the throttle forward to full power. The airplane sprang to life accelerating faster and faster. He no longer zigzagged for he had mastered the steering by now. Engine instruments in the green, all systems were go, the airspeed indicator bobbled to life, 40, 50, 60 knots (about 69 MPH) and he eased back on the controll yoke. The nose wheel lifted, then the mains, and he rose into the air pitching the nose toward the peak of the ridge off in the distance. He noticed that he was climbing rather quickly as the airplane performed much better now that he was alone. Although this flight would affirm his abilities, it was far more technical than pleasure. He would check and recheck himself the entire time. It was more of a test than a joy ride, but still his heart soared with the thought of what he was doing.

The altimeter read 1700 feet and he made his first left turn in the traffic pattern. Thoughts of his training started to run through his mind, "If I lost the engine now, I could easily glide to that field."

Another turn and he was level at two thousand feet, just a thousand feet above the ground. While retracting the flaps, he eased the power back a few hundred RPMs to the cruise setting. He kept a vigilant eye out for other airplanes as he announced his position over the radio. Looking down he could see Bill, Mr. Beichler as he respectfully referred to him, standing next to his dad by the old trailer. The two men were watching him patiently. With his wing abeam the approach end of the runway, he eased the power back once more and added flaps to help control the descent. The engine noise subsided a bit and he could hear the air rushing past the cockpit window. Another training flashback, "Always stay within gliding distance of the field." He turned again and added the second notch of flaps.

His heart started to race, this was it, all or nothing, hero or goat, it all came down to the landing. He started to whistle, softly at first then progressively louder. He rolled the wings level and aligned the airplane on the final approach course then added the final notch of flaps and made a minor power adjustment.

Easy, Chris thought, as the whistling subsided and his focus returned to the task at hand. He scanned the touchdown area making gentle corrections with the flight controls. His nervous jitters had been exchanged for pure concentration.

Chris crossed the runway threshold right on target and pulled the power to idle. A moment later he eased back gently on the stick, raising the nose, and holding the airplane just inches above the runway. He continued to ease back on the control yoke, looking to the end of the runway to judge his height. Easy, easy, he thought and...

The main wheels gently kissed the ground, then the nose and he rumbled softly down the center of the grass strip. He applied the brakes gently and cleared the runway at the first taxiway smiling confidently to himself in victory.

Adrenaline pumped through his system. He had done it. Chris had completed his first flight by himself and cleared the first big hurdle of his aviation career with the grace of an Olympic athlete. There was no more room for doubt. He was a pilot. A student pilot, but a pilot nonetheless. He was capable of safely carrying himself off into the sky and back again. What a feeling of accomplishment for a sixteen-year-old boy.

He returned to the beginning of the field and completed two more circuits. The next two were much more enjoyable and far less tense. Knowing his abilities, his confidence grew with every landing.

Chris got out of the airplane at the fuel pumps. Mr. Beichler greeted him with a handshake and a smile simply saying, "Excellent, excellent, you did great, Chris. I'll take care of the airplane, your dad is over there waiting to see you."

Chris' dad was beaming with pride as he grabbed and hugged him. "That was fantastic, absolutely fantastic! How do you feel?" Chris looked up smiling "That's the most fun I've ever had! It was great!"

They talked about the flight over lunch at Ferri's pizza parlor with the rest of the family. Chris was now the one being asked the questions as he shared the joy of his first solo. He celebrated with his family and Sue who had come with his mother and brother to meet them. Chris walked a little taller now, smiled a little brighter, beaming with pride in the first of many accomplishments along his path.

By
Michael A. Rencavage

7

The morning air was moist and fog lined the streets as Chris stood at the corner awaiting the paper truck. It was usually on time. He hoped that was the case today as he was anxious to start his deliveries. Chris pulled a breakfast bar from his paper bag and unwrapped it. He had just bitten into it and started to chew when the headlights of the paper truck pierced the morning fog. The driver didn't say a word. He simply threw the bundle of papers at Chris' feet and drove away with a nod that Chris took to mean good morning.

"Cash For Clunkers" read the headline in bold print. Chris rubbed his eyes, "What's that all about? he thought." He didn't realize it at first, but in the middle of an economic downturn, a well-intentioned government program was about to send his fathers' income into a spiral that would take years to recover from. The government offered large cash amounts in return for trading in your old gas guzzler and sending it off to the crusher. What they didn't realize is that they would inspire so many people to purchase new cars that it would completely disrupt the auto repair industry. Everyone was driving new cars and no one was fixing an old one. This put Christopher's father in a bad spot as business at the repair shop dwindled to the point that they had to let go of most of the mechanics. Chris' dad soon found himself out of work. Chris remembered that moment and the headline that started it all into motion.

Chris was in tune to the inevitability of the upcoming crisis as it approached. The day it all started to fall apart, the three-thirty bell was still resounding through the halls as Chris left the front door of the school. Anxious to get home, his feet raced across the pavement. If his dad was out of work for too long they stood a very real chance of losing the house. Chris was well aware of the family's financial situation. He knew there hadn't been much money left over each week after the bills were paid, and their savings account was all but non-existent. He couldn't help but feel a genuine concern for the well-being of his family.

54

Chris came in through the kitchen door, breathing heavily from his homeward dash. His father sat at the table with the sullen mood of the moment expressed clearly in his facial expression. Chris could feel the tension in the room as his mother poured a cup of coffee. His father began to speak in a soft voice, "I couldn't believe it. They didn't even let us finish the day. They just came in at noon and started passing out pink slips."

His father stood up and put his hands on the chair he had been sitting on. It wasn't characteristic of his father to show worry or concern, but this time it was very evident in his voice. "It will be all right, Chris, we'll just need to make a few adjustments around here, you know, minimize the spending until I can find work again. There are times when you just have to operate solely on faith. This is one of those times."

Chris was visibly concerned as he walked across the kitchen to get a drink of water. He questioned his father, "Is there anything I can do to help?" His father replied trying his hardest to be reassuring, "It will be fine, don't worry, we'll be just fine."

That night Chris sat alone on the limb of the apple tree beneath the autumn stars. The chill of the evening air reminded him that summer had ended as he pushed his hands into the pouch on the front of his sweatshirt. Looking up he gazed at the big dipper and the star shining brightly in the upper right corner of the cup. He thought of Sue and smiled.

He felt a little better after talking with his father, but his concerns were still haunting his thoughts. His family was now facing a tough time financially and he was quite aware of the effect that could have on them, not to mention the all but extinguishing of his dream.

He walked slowly down the path, then ran across the yard and down the road to Sue's house. He knew that if anyone in the world could understand his feelings it would be Sue.

They sat together talking for hours over hot cocoa and graham crackers. There really wasn't all that much that she could do for him. Still, the listening ear and friendly advice made Chris feel better. He left her house with a general feeling of hope for the future, knowing in his heart that it would all work out, somehow, someway.

Chris lay in bed that evening, prayers said, trying to focus on his dream. The tests seemed to be getting harder. Still he kept his dream alive following the directions Bob had given him. Eventually the thought of a future filled with happiness and dreams brought to life became sort of an escape for Chris. Perhaps there was really a light at the end of the tunnel. He couldn't see the light right now, but as his father had said, "There are times when you just have to operate solely on faith."

By
Michael A. Rencavage

8

Months had passed since the layoff. Chris' dad had absolutely no luck in finding a job as times were rough now for everyone in their small Pennsylvania town. His father tried to appear strong, but it was evident that this situation was really taking its toll on him, tearing hard at the very fabric of his spirit as he sold off everything that was not essential in an effort to just get by another month.

Chris' mom had sold off the rolls of silver coins she had been saving since she was a little girl. It had all come down to a matter of survival.

Their savings was depleted and the mortgage was due, regardless of the many attempts they had made to work something out with the bank. Chris knew it was only a matter of time until they would sell the house and move in with his grandparents. The house was special to their family. It was built by his uncle and every member of his family had pitched in during the construction. From his great-grandfather on down, the entire family invested their time and energy to make it someplace special. It truly hurt to see it lost to a time of financial strife for such a hard working group of people.

This house held a million memories, memories of joy and sadness that made the house special for him and his family. Now the only place Chris had ever lived, the storage place for all of his childhood memories, the birthplace of all his hopes and dreams was going to be sold to the highest bidder at auction as the bank reclaimed their just due.

Sometimes you just know beyond a shadow of a doubt the right thing to do. Chris was lying awake in bed, holding onto his dreamkeeper medallion, when it hit him like a ton of bricks.

The next morning Chris snuck into his parents room and stuffed the mortgage payment book into his backpack. On the way home from school he had completed his plan. He had stopped by the bank and withdrew the money from the sale of his motorcycle. With interest it was just enough for two months worth of mortgage payments and that is exactly what he used it for. It wouldn't solve the problem, but it would at least give the family a little more time, more time to hope and pray and work toward better days ahead.

That night he returned the payment book to the dresser in his parent's room and left the receipts on the table. He crawled into bed, happy with himself for having done something to ward off the impending trouble. He no longer felt as though there was a dragon breathing on his neck. He thought of something his father used to say, "Action of any kind always beats the fearful cowering of a victim of circumstance." Chris had swung the sword with all his might, the dragon had stumbled backward and they now had a little more time to find a permanent solution, together as a family.

By
Michael A. Rencavage

9

His parents were pleased with his act of kindness, not as much for the fact that it allowed them to keep the house, but more so because it showed the type of man that Chris was becoming. They thanked him and graciously promised to pay it back double when things got better.

Chris typically had Saturdays off at the grocery store. Ricky Johnson told Chris of a part time job bussing tables and doing dishes at the local banquet hall. Chris could work on Saturday nights to pick up a few extra dollars without hindering his school work. It was perfect. That day after school Chris and Ricky went to the banquet hall. Ricky introduced him to the boss and Chris took the job on a handshake and a promise.

Chris worked diligently Saturday after Saturday. Times were still tough for him and his family, but just as Bob had said, he never felt like a victim. This was merely something that had to be done. He even felt a little grateful that he had the opportunity to help his family. He pushed on through the tough times and kept his dream alive every night. In his spare time he would read his aviation books and run through the procedures of a flight in his mind, just to stay familiar with them.

One Saturday night when things were especially busy, Chris was bussing the tables and he ran into Mr. Carver, a guest at that evening's wedding celebration. Mr. Carver stood immediately and shook Chris' hand. "Where have you been, kid, don't like to fly anymore? I thought you were going to be a pilot." Chris explained his situation and Mr. Carver just nodded saying how sorry he was and wishing Chris better luck in the future. They shook hands once more and Chris returned to work as Mr. Carver rejoined the conversation at his table.

Later that night Chris and Ricky were working together, washing and drying the dishes after the wedding. Chris was going on and on to Ricky about his dream of becoming a professional pilot. His eyes glowed with excitement as he told his friend of the thrill of being at the controls of an airplane. Ricky listened intently to Chris describing his adventures to date.

Art was the head chef and supervisor of the kitchen help. He was tall, about six feet two inches, with salt and pepper hair and a belly that attested to his cooking. Art wasn't much for socializing, in fact he was rather quiet for the most part, except when he was barking orders to the staff. His lack of anything even closely related to a smile and his dark piercing eyes made him far more intimidating than friendly.

Art couldn't help but overhear the boys' conversation. He leaned toward them while he was walking by and said in his stern matter of fact tone, "Why don't you just give it up already, kid? That aviation business is for rich kids, it costs a fortune. Your family can barely afford to get by. What you should be concentrating on is finishing high school and going out to get a job that'll bring home some money." Art unrolled a pack of cigarettes from his shirt sleeve. "I can't stand you damn dreamers, talking your talk. In a year or so you'll be out of school and working. You'll see what the real world is like then." He huffed and walked out the back door to smoke.

The mood had changed to a post-confrontational quiet. Ricky looked at Chris, "Ignore him, he's just unhappy with his own life. His wife left him last year and he never gets to see his kids. He just can't stand to see anyone else happy." Chris dried the last dish, "He doesn't bother me. I know I'll make it. I simply won't stop trying until I do." He placed his hand on the medallion for a second then shut off the dishwasher and grabbed his coat. He turned off the lights and followed Ricky out the back door into the cold winter night. They walked home together with their hands in their pockets, their warm breath rising like smoke from their mouths.

It was eleven-thirty when Chris got home and by eleven-thirty-one he had heard the good news. It wasn't just good news, it was great news. Christopher's dad was to start first thing Monday morning at his new job. It seems as though the local university had developed a need for a director of maintenance. The position suited his dad quite well and the pay and benefits would be even better than what he had earned as a mechanic. Chris was beaming with joy at the news.

He was so happy for his dad and his entire family that he almost missed a very important part of the conversation. Working at the university entitled anyone in the family to a free education. Chris would be able to go to college and make one of the most important steps toward the realization of his dream. He couldn't believe how well things were coming together, it seemed as though it just couldn't get any better than this. That is until the phone call came at eight a.m. the following morning. It was Mr. Carver and he asked Chris to be at the airport by nine o'clock. His tone seemed joyful as he stressed that it was very important.

The minivan didn't even have time to warm up, Chris was at the airport in minutes. It was a cold December day, clear and calm, but cold. Chris looked to see if anyone was flying on the approach to the airport. One airplane cast a shadow over the road as he sat with his turn signal blinking on route 435. He was anxious to find out exactly what was so important that Mr. Carver had called him and asked for a meeting.

He made the corner and slid a little on the gravel of Airport drive then eased the minivan up alongside the old trailer. When he got there Mr. Carver was pumping gas into one of the flight school airplanes. He saw Chris standing next to the stairs as he packed away the fuel hose. He walked over and firmly shook Chris' hand. "I didn't say you had to rush right over, but I like your enthusiasm. Let's go inside for a minute."

Mr. Carver sat in a chair by the television grabbing a model airplane from the table in front of him. He sat there spinning the propeller and started to speak. "I've been talking with Mr. Beichler and your dad. They both assured me of your sincerity in pursuing a career as a pilot. You do understand that it can be a pretty tough road at times?" Chris replied respectfully, " Yes sir I do." Mr. Carver continued, " In the end though the reward far outweighs the sacrifice. I made my career as an aviator and I can safely say that I look back now with very few regrets. That's why I want to help you."

Chris started to smile as Mr. Carver continued. "Here's the deal. I'll let you complete your ratings for free. You in exchange will work here nights and weekends at the going rate until you have paid me back in full. You'll have to work as much as possible without interfering with your studies. You'll get a real chance to pursue your dream and I'll get a valuable employee I can count on. Does that sound fair to you?" Chris was shocked. He couldn't speak for a minute. He unconsciously reached for his medallion as he replied with a slight crackle in his voice, "That sounds great! When can I start?" "Right after your next flight lesson, Mr. Beichler's waiting for you on the flight line." Chris jumped to his feet grinning from ear to ear as he shook Mr. Carver's hand. "I don't know how to thank you." "Just do a good job and become a good pilot, that's all I ask," said Mr. Carver. Chris raced out the door to meet his flight instructor.

Michael A. Rencavage

By
Michael A. Rencavage

10

The first rays of morning light bounced off the high stratus layer of clouds creating a magenta glow that illuminated the eastern sky. The checklist complete, Chris turned to Sue and asked if she was ready. As she replied, he depressed the small silver button. The little Lycoming engine roared to life, empowering the Piper Cherokee he had rented to fly his first passenger since receiving his private license.

After nearly three years he was now able to fulfill the promise he had made beneath the apple tree. He taxied slowly toward the beginning of the runway for a northeast departure. Sue sat next to him smiling, excited and maybe just a little nervous. He finished the final checks and glanced at Sue as he called on the radio, "November 7203 Juliet taking the active runway for immediate departure."

He smoothly added full power and aligned the airplane with the runway. The propeller spun so fast that it was all but invisible as it blasted the last droplets of morning dew from the windshield.

Engine instruments in the green, the airspeed indicator bobbled to life and they quickly accelerated to reach the airplanes flying speed. With gentle back pressure on the stick they were gradually transformed from helpless subjects of gravity to a giant soaring aluminum bird destined for the sky.

The sun brilliantly reflected in the deep maroon cowling of the aircraft's nose and they were lifted together on the calm morning air, gently climbing higher and higher. At thirty-five hundred feet, Chris eased back on the power and they leveled off. Beneath them lay all of the beauty that the world had to offer. Fields of emerald and gold swayed softly in the gentle morning breeze. The crystal lakes of Pennsylvania, pools of rippling sunlight, floated gently past. Sue's mind flashed to a scene from Aladdin where the princess was whisked away for a view of her world that she had never experienced before. It was glorious and majestic as Chris banked to the left, slicing the azure sky with ivory wings.

He swooped down for a closer look at their hometown. They passed the church and the supermarket, then Sue's house and then Chris'. It was almost surreal, just five hundred feet above the ground it all looks so different. It's cleaner, more pure from the air. The whole world takes on a different perspective.

Up ahead and to the south the morning sun was reflected in the valley fog, pockets of luminescent gold among emerald hills. "It's magical," said Sue as they climb once more. Chris put the airplane through a graceful aerial ballet as he practiced the maneuvers he must perform for his commercial rating, smooth and gentle climbs and dives, tilting and twisting the world to his liking. Sue had felt the freedom he had felt, she had seen the beauty he had seen, and now she knew why this dream had become so important to him.

Sue heard the grass blades as they flickered softly against the wheels, then the muffled rumble of tire on grass as Chris settled the airplane gently to the runway. They taxied to the pump and shut down. While getting out, Chris handed the keys and clipboard to the next person waiting to rent the airplane. As they walked down the drive to Sue's car she laid her head on Chris' shoulder. "That was magnificent!" she said. Then she stopped... and kissed him, "What a great day."

69

By
Michael A. Rencavage

11

The cockpit was pitch black. Flying inside a thick layer of clouds in the middle of the night the view was not unlike looking out from the inside of a bottle of black ink. The only light was provided by the hundreds of knobs and dials in the cockpit, each one with a specific purpose. Chris set cruise power and called for the checklist at the leisure of the darkened silhouette working beside him. It was quiet for a moment, not even a call from air traffic control.

The darkened cockpit was suddenly invaded by flashing red lights. *"Chris the number two engine is on fire!"* ,said the first officer in a calm but firm voice. Chris replied, "We're going to have to shut it down." "Place your hand on the number two power lever." The tension level in the cockpit rose, the emergency was serious. An engine fire could easily ignite the fuel tank with disastrous results. They needed to act quickly and correctly.

First officer: " Confirm"

Chris glanced to be sure his first officer's hand was on the appropriate lever, a matter of procedure designed to prevent inadvertent worsening of the situation. This would be done before the execution of each command in this type of emergency.

Chris: " Flight idle. Place your hand on the engine2 shut off button." Chris increased the power on the number one engine and added a little rudder and trim to keep flying straight and level.

First officer: "Confirm"

Chris: Off. " Place your hand on the fire bottle A switch."

First officer: "Confirm"

Chris: "Fire the A extinguish bottle and start the timer. Run the engine fire in flight checklist. I'll talk to ATC."

Chris declared an emergency with air traffic control and turned the airplane toward the Philadelphia International Airport. He then called the flight attendant to brief her on the emergency.

First officer: "Thirty seconds and we're still on fire!"

Chris: "Fire the B extinguish bottle."

Descending now and heading for the runway they were still in the clouds. The weather had closed in at Philadelphia, the clouds were low and the visibility was poor. It was the very minimum allowed for landing.

Still eight miles out, unable to see anything out the cockpit window, Chris had an escalating problem on his hands. They had fired both extinguishers and the fire was still burning on the right engine. Chris had one chance and one chance only to bring himself, his crew and the passengers to safety. That is as long as the fire didn't ignite one of the fuel tanks and bring it all to a sudden end. If they couldn't break out of the clouds and see the runway, there would never be enough time to go back up and try again as the flames would simply engulf the aircraft before they could make another attempt at landing. Chris had to be right on during his approach. The outcome rested firmly in his hands. Still Chris remained calm.

Flying by the instruments he called, "flaps 1". The first officer complied, He slowed to 160 knots, "Gear down, flaps 2, again the first officer complied. Slowing once more toward the final approach speed Chris called, "flaps full , before landing checklist." They completed the final items of their checklist. The first officer monitored their progress. "One thousand above." At 500 feet above minimums, he called the speed and decent rate then gave the signal to the flight attendant to get the passengers in the brace position. Moments that seemed like hours later the first officer called, "Two hundred above, one hundred above, at minimums, still no contact." A thick fog had rolled in bringing the clouds right down to the runway surface.

They were still descending and less than two-hundred feet in the air, with no sight of the runway they were supposed to land on and their right engine engulfed in flames. Their navigation instruments could not be relied upon this close to the ground. They could end up touching down anywhere without accurate guidance and a landing made off of the runway could be very dangerous. They however, had no choice, they had to land whether they could see or not. Chris continued, more focused than ever. He tried to slow their descent to ease the impact, sweat dripping from his brow.

"Chris we're just about fifty feet above the ground, "said the first officer.' "Twenty feet, Ten feet......."

74

CRASH!...the airplanes main wheels smacked hard onto the runway. Chris struggled to see the lines and keep the airplane straight through the fog, racing down the runway at over 100 miles per hour. He pulled the power levers back and over the gate into reverse thrust and stepped hard on the brakes In seconds they were stopped. The emergency vehicles were awaiting their arrival as per their request. Chris gave the first officer the evacuation instructions as he shut down the airplane.

"Nice job guys, looks like you passed another one," said the voice from behind them. The simulator door swung open and they squinted as their eyes adjusted to the flood of fluorescent light.

By
Michael A. Rencavage

12

Al held the door for Chris as they left the pilot training facility. "So how are Sue and the kids?" "Great", said Chris. "In fact, they're picking me up here at five o'clock and we're heading to the airport. Martine wants to fly the Cub for a while. I think we'll head over to Blairstown for a burger. That'll get us back around eight o'clock to rendezvous with Sue and Molly." Al opened his car door and got inside. The window opened as he cranked. "Sounds like a great time, have fun." He started the car and pulled away.

Sue pulled in just moments later. Chris jumped in and leaned over to kiss his wife. They had been married for fifteen years by now and had a happy marriage with two great kids. Martine was tall and thin but strong, 14 years old and smart as a whip. She loved to ride around their property and the local dirt roads on her little Honda motorcycle. It was her transportation, but she loved that bike. As the ad said, "You meet the nicest people on a Honda." Martine was kind and funny and she lit up a room just by walking in the door, the nicest people indeed. With auburn hair and hazel eyes, she was a beautiful young lady, but she was a tomboy at heart who loved to spend time with her dad. They did everything together, What Martine loved most, however, was flying in the old Piper Cub with Chris.

Molly was ten years old. She was quiet and polite and also extremely intelligent with a well-developed love for science and reading. She loved to spend time with her mom and grandmother. That was their plan today. After dropping off Martine and Chris, they were going to her grandparent's house to help them plant their garden and visit for a while.

They dropped the intrepid aviators at the airport then drove away down the dusty road that lead back to the highway. Chris and Martine walked to their hangar. The huge steel doors were painted yellow, faded and chipped from years of service. They brought to mind scenes of an old warehouse that had been forgotten for years. Chris opened the hangar doors, the rollers squeaked and squealed, cold steel on pavement.

In the evening with the sun setting in the west it was always a dramatic event to open these doors. The sunlight filled the hangar unveiling the treasures within. The jewel of this discovery sat sparkling in the middle of the floor. N9645J always looked so proud, the lemon -yellow Piper Cub with its nose pointed to the sky as if it knew where it belonged. Chris loved this airplane and so did Martine. They had spent many evenings sailing through the sky together in the Cub and it was special to them because of those memories. Chris wondered how many other people had cherished the wonderful old airplane.

Flying since 1946 it was older than Chris. He had bought it and restored it some 14 years ago hoping to share it someday with his newborn daughter. They pulled it from the hangar together.

The sun glistened on the meticulously polished fabric of the Cub yellow wings. Chris always thought it funny that this airplane, one of the slowest airplanes still flying, had a racy black lightning bolt painted down each side. But that was the original paint scheme and in keeping with tradition that was how he wanted it.

Martine crawled in the cockpit and held the brakes. Chris called out, "Mags off", "Mags off," Martine replied. Chris pulled the propeller around by hand three or four times. These airplanes were so simplistic by design that they didn't even have electric starters. Chris yelled, "Mags on." Martine replied, "Mags on." Chris reached up to grab the prop,

"All right Martine , hold the brakes as hard as you can." He swung the prop with all his might, stepping back out of the way.

The little engine coughed, then sputtered, then chugged to life, eventually smoothing out as it came up to speed. Chris ran around the side and pulled the chocks from the tires. He jumped in and they taxied down the path to the grass runway, making gentle s-turns back and forth so that they could see what was in front of them.

All the checks complete, Chris taxied into position for takeoff. "All right, Martine, you've got the controls," he yelled. Martine loved to fly. She had been flying with her dad for as long as she could remember. Martine added power. She pressed in just a little right rudder as they accelerated down the runway. The tail started to fly first as Martine added gentle forward pressure on the stick, lifting the tail wheel from the ground. "Nice and easy," yelled Chris over the storm of air rushing in through the open window and door of the Cub. Martine eased back on the stick and the little yellow Cub stepped softly into the sky. She raised the nose and climbed slowly away from the ground. They flew away off to the east on evening air as smooth as glass, not a bump, not a ripple in the sky that night.

Chris yelled once more from the rear cockpit, "I have the controls." Martine shook the stick gently in acknowledgment. Chris had been flying now for quite a few years. He had thousands and thousands of hours in his log book, but he still loved to fly. This was the type of flying he loved the most. Sharing an evening sky with his daughter in an airplane that was so simple by design that it returned him to the reasons he had started to fly in the first place. The joy of flight, the freedom of flight, the pure fun of flying.

The Cub chugged along at only sixty-five miles per hour, barely keeping pace with the cars on the interstate below. Its door and window were designed to be able to be kept open in flight, and that is how they kept it as they enjoyed the panoramic view of the countryside and tasted the cool clear air at altitude. Flying just five hundred feet above the rural towns, they could see every detail of the landscape. The cars, the people, all bustling below as they sailed along carefree in the evening sky.

Chris said to Martine, "Watch this!" He climbed then banked sharply to the left, lemon wings circled the cottonball cloud but never touched it. Martine felt as though she could reach out and grab it. Chris continued to play. Nose down he raced beneath the cloud, the windshield filled with fields of gold and green, then quickly back on the stick, full power, and azure sky was all that Martine could see. Up and over the top of the cloud and down the other side. The world was right again and they cruised toward the shimmering lake at the top of the ridge.

Chris gave the controls back to Martine and they descended once more toward the river valley as the peaks of the gorge rose to meet their wings on either side. A gentle bank to the east and rising in their windshield was their destination. Martine eased the Cub into the traffic pattern. Abeam the runway she pulled the power to idle and the mild roar of the engine gave way to the sound of rushing air as she glided the airplane to a perfect three-point landing and they taxied to the ramp in front of the restaurant.

Chris cut the engine and they got out together. Blairstown was always one of Chris' favorite airports. There was a glider school, a flight school, and a great little restaurant on the field. What he liked most about it though was that it possessed a certain quality that brought back memories of the way aviation used to be. There were no corporate jets or airliners, the field was so small that they could never land there. It was rural, set out in the country next to the ridge. People from the town would come out for dinner and enjoyed watching the little airplanes take-off and land. It was rather ideal, possessing all of the modern conveniences, but with a classic charm. There was evidence of that charm everywhere. Looking around the field you could see more classic airplanes than at any other airport in the state. People came here from all over.

They had eaten dinner, a true gourmet delicacy of burgers and fries, topped off with a milkshake. As they were pre-flighting the airplane, Chris checked the oil and thought it best that they add a quart before leaving. Chris and Martine walked around the side of the hangar toward the maintenance shop. Chris was awestruck, he couldn't believe it! It had been hidden on the other side of the ramp blocked from view by the hangar. He looked away and back again. That was it he thought. No doubt that's it. The huge radial engine, the cloud white wings with gold and silver trim. It looked exactly like it did twenty-five years ago, twenty-five years to the day Chris thought as he looked at the date on his watch.

The tall muscular man came out from behind the left wing. He was a little older looking, gray hair grown out a bit but still neat and business like. He was wiping his hands with the polishing cloth when his dark inset eyes met Chris'. "Bob? Bob Speranza? I met you twenty-five years ago when your airplane made a forced landing in the field next to my house."

Bob smiled, "I remember, how could I forget? You know that engine never quit before and never quit since, must have been meant to be. How

82

are you? What are you up to these days?" They sat at the old picnic table outside of the hangar and talked for quite a while. Chris told him about all of the wonderful things he had done in his life.

Chris said, "I could never forget you. You changed my life. You gave me the dreamkeeper medallion and it empowered me, it made my dreams come true one after another until now I find myself in a life that is far better than anything I could ever have imagined back then."

Bob asked, "Do you still have it? The medallion that is." "I sure do," replied Chris and he called Martine over from the soda machine across the hangar. He took the medallion from Martine's neck and handed it to Bob. It had a few dings in it since the last time he had seen it, but Bob was pleasantly surprised.

He studied it carefully holding it in his hand. "My grandfather gave me this, it always meant a lot to me growing up. I see that you've used it quite a bit, but have you unlocked its secret?" Chris stumbled for a moment, "I uh, I think I understand how it works." Bob held the medallion in his hand as he pulled a tiny pen knife from his pocket. He took it and twisted a slotted disc on the back, then wedged the pen knife in an almost imperceptible seam along the medallions bottom edge. It opened like a clam shell in his hand. "This is the key to all its power," Bob said and he passed it carefully to Chris. Looking inside Chris saw himself reflected in a tiny mirror.

Bob went on, "The true power of the medallion lies within you. It is you that made your dreams come true, your prayers and your hard work. When my grandfather explained the powers of the medallion to me he quoted an old saying, "Great ideas must have landing gear as well as wings." That is what you've done, you've kept the faith, working hard in good times and in bad and you have been rewarded as such." Bob wiped the medallion with the polishing cloth and handed it back to Martine, then turned toward Chris once more. "The rewards were simple at first, being able to see a brighter future during a harsh time in your life. They later became more evident as your life began to emulate your dreams and your reality had changed accordingly. The medallion was merely a tool to help a young boy hold fast to his dreams. You've done a good job my friend, a very good job indeed."

That night Chris walked into Martine's moonlit room. He leaned over the edge of the top bunk and kissed his sleeping daughter goodnight. Looking at the medallion clasped tightly in his young daughter's hand, he wondered what dreams had eased her off to sleep?

The End

Acknowledgements

I wanted to take a moment and thank my wife Judi. She is always supportive of my endeavors and she is the love of my life. Thank you to Christopher and Mikey for being wonderful sons and a blessing and inspiration. Thank you to Taylor and Patrick, although step sons by technicality and to not be disrespectful to their real father who is a good dad to his boys, they are my family as well and they have been such a blessing to my life.

The story I have presented here has reflections in not just my personal path to becoming an aviator, but from discussions with many others who I have flown with and come to know over the years. Thank you to those who have inspired and encouraged me and outright helped me along the way. Thank you, Mr. Robert Seamans of Seamans airport, similar to Mr. Carver in the story, Bob Seamans actually pulled me aside and let me run an interest free tab flying as frequently as I liked to get my private license at a time when I could only afford to fly once every month or two. He kept my dream alive. I promptly repaid him. Shortly after becoming a private pilot, a job opportunity in the medical equipment field doubled my salary providing more opportunity and the chance to partner in an airplane. Thank you to Bill Beichler an amazing man of so many skills and true intellect and also my primary flight instructor. A big thank you to the Scrobola family of Valley Aviation in Forty-fort Pa. Jimmy, Joyce, Charles and Joey have been friends and mentors as they are the first family of aviation in the Scranton-Wilkes barre area. Reading the book, the name Bob Speranza stands out. That is chosen for a reason as Bob Charette and Dave Speranza helped me so much in my quest to change careers and do what I love. Bob Speranza shares characteristics of both of these fine men who I am honored to call my friends for decades, many decades. I have to thank Patrick Flannery as well. Another decades long friendship, Pat has brought such insight and inspiration to my life. Thank you all.

Thank you to Flexjet management and personnel in every facet of the company who help the pilots every single day in so many ways. Thank you to all of the pilots of the committees I've served on who gave of their time for the betterment of the pilot group and the company. Especially John Huppe and J.C. Krueger , Terry Thomson, Mark Morgan and so many others. Thank you to each and every pilot I have had the pleasure of sharing a cockpit with, too many to mention here.

Special thanks to team423, my current coworkers and good friends Martine Davis and Derek Curlee. You are both amazing!

Thank you to Flexjet my employer for a great job that surrounds me with great people and keeps my passion for flying alive.

Thank you, the reader, for buying my book and visiting awhile while I tell my tale and practice a new craft, the written word holds my heart. I hope it holds yours as well and that you enjoyed the ride, perhaps even found a word or two of inspiration along the way. I am a dreamer and an optimist over all, I hope you keep your dreams alive and tend to the flame so as to live a full and rewarding life.

Godspeed, Mike

About the Author

Mike Rencavage is a professional aviator with thirty years of flying experience; having held positions as a flight instructor and pilot for both general aviation and the airlines. He is currently a corporate pilot for Flexjet LLC out of Cleveland, Ohio. Flexjet is one of the nation's premier fractional ownership companies. He is the father of two amazing young men Michael K (Mikey) Rencavage and Christopher Joseph Rencavage. His blended family is completed with his wife Judi and her two sons Patrick and Taylor. He was born and raised in Scranton, Pennsylvania and now resides in Dallas, Pa.

Mike has authored three books and been published several times in magazines and journals in the fields of aviation and rehabilitation engineering. (A former career path) He loves family and friends and all things aviation. He and his wife Judi are avid motorcyclists and enjoy hiking on the great trails throughout Pennsylvania, Virginia, West Virginia and the Carolinas.

Please take a few minutes and rate and review "Dreamkeeper".

Just go to amazon.com and put **"Rencavage books"** in the search engine. Select **"Dreamkeeper"** and scroll to the review section.

<u>Or just use the QR code below on your phone's camera.</u>

Scroll down to the "Write a review" block near the bottom.

Made in the USA
Middletown, DE
09 December 2022

17797760R00051